Chris Passey & Siobhan King

Millie's Socks

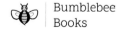

Bumblebee Books

www.olympiapublishers.com
OLYMPIA PAPERBACK EDITION

A CIP catalogue record for this title is
available from the British Library.

ISBN: 978-1-83934-442-8

This is a work of fiction.
Names, characters, places and incidents originate from the writer's imagination.
Any resemblance to actual persons, living or dead, is purely coincidental.

First Published in 2023

Olympia Publishers
Tallis House
2 Tallis Street
London
EC4Y 0AB

Printed in Great Britain

Dedication

Chris

To Attiye - nakupenda mpenzi wangu

For Kimichi School & Maddie - thank you for the inspiration; always be you.

For Luna & Zachary - keep reading and keep believing.

Siobhan

For Lily from Auntie Siobhan

In a normal town, during normal times, a girl named Millie lives with her Mom in a normal house.

But that is the only normal thing about Millie. You see, Millie sees the world differently to her friends.

Her brain is extraordinary and far from normal. And Millie quite likes it that way.

'Who wants to be normal anyway?' she would say to her Mom.

'Quite right!' would always be the reply from Millie.

Most of the time, Millie's brain can feel like there's rain always falling inside.

This rain can be heavy and make it difficult to see people's faces properly and to understand

what they are feeling. Sometimes, this rain can be so heavy that it mixes with the butterflies in her

tummy and causes a huge storm that rushes through her body and makes her confused and upset.

Sometimes, it's really hard being Millie but her friends at school always try to make her feel better.

Mondays at school were usually quite boring for Millie, especially if it was raining hard inside her brain.

Millie was **miserable** in Maths

She was **sad** through Science

Millie **failed** at football

And **cried** in Choir.

Millie got so upset that Miss. Lorna had to suggest she took some time to calm down in the

Chillout Den where Millie could breathe, relax and try and quieten the rain in her brain.

Just like you, Millie loves lots of different things in her life:

She loves reading **fantasy books**

She loves **spicy food**

And she loves **watching football** with her mom

But, more than anything in the world, Millie **loves SOCKS.**

Stripey, spotty, **odd**, long, **short**, holey, **funny**.

Each morning before school, Millie likes to look through every pair of socks to decide

which ones she will wear that day. She thinks about how they might feel,

how they might look and how they make her feel.

One gloomy Monday morning, a very gloomy Millie was beginning her **Sock Choosing Ritual**

as she did every morning. It was raining outside but it was also raining inside Millie's brain.

She thought that picking the right pair of socks might make her feel better.

She placed them all on the floor and began to choose.

Spotty? No, not today; too scratchy.

Stripey? No, not these ones either, she didn't like the colour today.

Then, out of the corner of her eye she saw a pair of socks she had never seen before.

They were long black and red football socks.

Millie reached out and let her fingertips touch the woolly sock. Millie gasped. It was the

softest sock she had ever felt. She put them on and stood up. Millie felt **AMAZING.**

The rain inside her head stopped and she felt **calm** and ... and ... **SUPER!**

Millie ran downstairs in her new socks.

'Morning Mom!' she screamed. Her Mom jumped up from the sofa, her jam on toast flying everywhere.

'Goodness Millie, you're excited this morning'. Her Mom smiled and gave Millie a massive hug.

Millie proudly pointed to her feet, 'New socks; new me ... byeeeeee!'

Millie's voice faded into the distance as she ran out of the door and up the hill to school,

happier than she had been in a long time. As we know, Mondays were usually

quite boring for Millie but today was different.

Millie **mastered** her **Maths** work.

She **smashed** her **science** lesson.

Powered through **PE**

And even **conquered choir.**

For the first time in a very long time, the rain in her brain and the butterflies in her tummy were quiet.

'It's definitely the socks' Millie told her Mom over her favourite spicy curry that night.

'I'm sure it is Mills,' her Mom laughed.

'I even did some singing today!' Millie continued as she got up from the table

and swished around the kitchen, jumped over a chair and ran upstairs.

When she got to her room, Millie took off her socks and threw them into the corner where all of the washing goes.

Millie had a shower, read some of her favourite fantasy book and — finally — got into bed.

Millie lay there in the moonlight, her brain calm and her eyes closing ... wondering what amazing

adventures she and her socks might have tomorrow.

The next morning, the sun woke Millie up. She sat up and immediately ran to her sock drawer,

emptying the contents and preparing herself for the **Sock Choosing Ritual.**

Stripey, spotty, **odd,** long, **short,** holey, **funny** ... Millie was struggling to choose.

'I could wear the black and red socks again?' Millie said out loud.

No one replied, so she ran over to the washing pile but it wasn't there.

The socks were gone! Millie frantically searched her room, socks flying everywhere,

but she couldn't find her long black and red football socks.

'MO-OOM! WHERE ARE MY SOCKS?' Millie screamed as she ran downstairs.

'I put them in the wash, Millie. You can't wear socks two days in a row!'

'WHY?!' Millie wept staring at the washing machine and a spinning blur of black and red inside.

'Because no one will play football with a Millie with STINKY feet!'

Her Mom was laughing at the thought of Millie's smelly feet because of dirty socks.

Some adults actually think like this. How boring!

Millie started to get really upset, the rain in her head started gently falling

and she felt some of it begin to fill her eyes.

'YOU'VE RUINED EVERYTHING!' Millie wept as she grabbed her school bag,

shoved on her shoes and ran out of the house, into the rain and up the hill towards school.

She had left the house so quickly that she had forgotten to wear any socks at all

Millie's Tuesday did not start well.

She had a **meltdown** in **maths** and soon found herself in the Chillout Den,

trying to calm the storm in her head and quieten the butterflies in her tummy.

Millie's teacher, Miss Lorna, gently knocked on the Den door. She popped her head into the room.

'You've had such a good few days, Millie. What on earth is wrong?' Miss Lorna asked,

sitting next to her on the bed in the Den. Millie struggled to find the words at first,

the rain made it hard to hear her own thoughts. She took a deep breath and tried to concentrate.

'I found some socks that made me a superhero and my Mom washed them

and now I'm just plain old Millie again ...' she began to cry heavily again.

'Wow. Super hero socks, eh? Were they those black and red football ones?' Millie nodded slowly.

'But today you have **NO** socks on' Millie nodded again.

'**Oh MY!** Your feet are going to be very smelly!'

Millie let out a little smile. 'I didn't mind' she said innocently.

'Tell you what,' Miss Lorna began, 'Make sure you come to football club at lunch

and I'll try to sort something out for you.'

Millie sighed, 'I can't play football. Not without my socks'.

'Millie, you don't need those socks to be a superhero or a footballer. You're fantastic all on your own.'

Miss Lorna smiled at Millie who could just about make out the twinkle in her eyes

as the sound of the rain in her head began to get quieter. Miss Lorna left Millie in the Den to

gather her thoughts and to wonder what awaited her at Football club.

When the lunch bell rang, Millie's heart began to race.

She walked towards the football pitch where she could see all of her classmates gathered around Miss Lorna.

The rain in her head began to fall again and Millie slowed down. 'I can't do this,' she said out loud.

The rain fell even harder inside and the football pitch started to become fuzzy and fade away.

Then Millie remembered what Miss Lorna had said,

'Millie, you don't need those socks to be a superhero or a footballer. You're fantastic all on your own.'

'No, I CAN do this.'

The rain in her brain started to slow down and Millie began to see the football pitch again.

Her friends and Miss Lorna were all standing in front of her and Maddie could clearly see them all smiling.

'Millie,' Miss Lorna stepped forward, 'Your friends would like to help you feel like a superhero again.'

And at that, her friends each held out a **brand new, CLEAN** pair of **black and red football socks!**

'One for every day of the month!' Millie cried, '**thank you so much!**'

Millie kicked her shoes off and took a pair of socks. She remembered how soft they felt

in her hands and quickly put them on over her feet, pulling them right up to just below her knees.

Miss Lorna rolled the football to Millie's feet and Millie, a superhero once more,

kicked the first kick of the match and had an amazing day.

That night, Millie was swishing around the kitchen again. Her Mom tapped her on the shoulder.

'Sorry for washing your socks, Mills. I didn't realise how important they were to you.'

'It's OK Mom!' Millie took her socks off and put them in the washing machine. Her Mom's face was a picture!

'So I can wash these can I?'

'Yep!' said Millie, swishing up the stairs.

'And you won't be upset?'

'No Mom,' Millie paused on the landing, 'I'm a superhero with or without my socks.'

'Ok lovely,' her Mom laughing, a little bit confused, 'Love you Mills.'

'Love you Mom … byyeeeeeee!' Millie jumped into her room, closed the door and dove into bed.

Before she fell asleep, Millie looked over to the sock drawer now BURSTING with black and red football socks.

'Well,' she said aloud, 'Sock Choosing Ritual will be MUCH faster from now on!'

About the Author

Chris Passey is an educator and creative professional from the West Midlands. As Deputy Head and SENDCo at Kimichi School Independent Music School in Birmingham, Chris works with remarkable and amazing young people, just like Millie, every day. Chris lives in Bromsgrove with his wife, Attiye and is a Fellow of The Royal Society of Arts (RSA).

Acknowledgements

My eternal gratitude to my wife Attiye and to my incredible illustrator Siobhan for joining me in this amazing journey. Thank you to my Mom for reading to me every day and fostering a love of reading and books that has led directly to Millie's Socks.